CONTENTS

Glossary

 **beanbag toss** a game where you take turns throwing beanbags into a container

 **egg-and-spoon race** a race between teams in which each person carries an egg on a spoon, then passes it to the next team member's spoon

 **hula-hoop** a large plastic ring that you spin around your body by moving your hips in circles

 **three-legged race** a race between teams of two people who are standing side by side with their inner legs tied together

KIDS' SPORT STORIES

SPORTS DAY RULES!

by Cari Meister

illustrated by Seb Burnett

raintree

a Capstone company — publishers for children

9112000473840

Raintree is an imprint of Capstone Global Library Limited, a company incorporated in England and Wales having its registered office at 264 Banbury Road, Oxford, OX2 7DY – Registered company number: 6695582

www.raintree.co.uk
myorders@raintree.co.uk

ISBN 978 1 3982 1495 8

Designed by Kyle Grenz
Originated by Capstone Global Library Ltd
Printed and bound in India

British Library Cataloguing in Publication Data
A full catalogue record for this book is available from the British Library.

Chapter 1

RAIN OR SHINE

It was almost time for school to start. Raj took off his wet raincoat and shook it out. Just then, his friend Gigi walked past.

"Raj!" she said. "Watch out!"

"Sorry!" Raj said.

"It's OK," she said, smiling. "It's only a bit of water."

"Can you believe it's raining?" a voice said. It was their classmate Stan. "And today is sports day! How are we going to have sports day in the rain?"

Raj shrugged. "Maybe we'll have it in the hall," he said.

Stan frowned. "In the hall?" he said. "That won't be any fun."

Raj, Gigi and Stan walked together to their classroom and sat down. Another classmate, Tess, was already at their table.

"I hope sports day isn't cancelled," Gigi said sadly.

"Rain or shine," Tess said.

"What does that mean?" asked Stan.

"Sports day will happen, even if it's raining," Tess explained. "If it rains, we'll be in the hall."

"Oh no," Stan said. "Being stuck in the hall won't work at all. Rain, rain, go away!"

But the rain didn't go away. So Raj and his classmates headed to the hall.

Once they got there, Mr Winters handed each pupil a large plastic hoop.

"Our first sports-day game today is the hula-hoop," Mr Winters said. "Whoever keeps the hoop spinning around their body the longest wins."

"I'm great at this!" Stan said. "I'll definitely win!"

But keeping the hoop spinning was a lot harder than it looked. Stan didn't win.

To his surprise, Raj won. Gigi high-fived her friend.

"Nice job, Raj!" she said.

Raj grinned. "I practised," he said.

Chapter 2

PAIRED UP

The beanbag toss was next. "Try to throw all five beanbags into the bucket," Mr Winters said.

Stan pushed to the front of the queue.

"I'll go first!" he shouted. "I'll show everyone how to do it."

The other kids watched Stan throw all
five beanbags into the bucket.

"See?" he said. "I'm the best."

Gigi went next. She got one beanbag in. Raj got three. Tess got all five!

"Awesome!" Stan said to Tess. "I hope we're partners later for the pairs game. We'll beat everyone!"

Gigi poked Raj. "I hope Stan isn't my partner," she said quietly. "I'm not good at pairs games. He would get cross if we lost."

Raj squeezed Gigi's hand. "Don't worry," he said. "Remember, they're only games."

Just then, Mr Winters opened the big hall doors.

"The rain has stopped!" he said. "Let's move the rest of the games outside. What do all of you think?"

The kids cheered.

"Perfect!" Mr Winters said. "Sports day really is best outside."

Then he pulled out a list. "But first, let me tell you who your partner is for the pairs games."

Gigi crossed her fingers. She hoped she would get Raj.

But she didn't. Raj got Tess. Gigi got Stan.

"This is bad," Gigi said to Raj.

"The games are supposed to be fun," Raj said. "It doesn't matter who wins."

"Stan doesn't feel that way," Gigi said as everyone walked outside.

Chapter 3
A FUN MESS

It may have stopped raining, but now the field was super muddy. During the sack race, Raj slipped and fell. Then Tess and two other kids did too. They couldn't help but laugh at the mess!

Gigi started to giggle. Stan shook his head.

"We are going to beat everyone in the pairs games," he told her.

Soon everyone was tied to their partner for the three-legged race. Mr Winters blew his whistle. The race began.

Stan and Gigi had an early lead. But Stan tried to go too fast. Gigi tripped, and the two of them fell. They lost to Raj and Tess.

"I'm sorry, Stan," Gigi said.

Stan didn't say anything.

The final game was the egg-and-spoon race. It was going to be extra tough with the muddy field.

"You'll be slower, so you start," Stan told Gigi. "I can make up the time you lose."

Gigi got her spoon and egg. Mr Winters blew his whistle, and the race began.

"Run, Gigi! Run!" Stan yelled.

Gigi didn't run. She walked. And she kept the egg on the spoon! Other kids dropped their eggs and had to start again.

Gigi was in the lead when she passed the egg to Stan. Now it was Stan's turn to take over and win.

Stan started to run, but his foot slipped
in the mud. He landed hard. So did the egg!

It landed right on Stan's head.

Gigi ran over to help him up.

"You must be so cross with me," Stan said. "I made us lose."

"I'm not cross at all!" said Gigi.

"Really?" Stan asked.

"Really!" Gigi said. "I had fun. That's what sports day is all about."

Stan wiped his face and smiled. "Fun and lots of egg slime," he said.

Raj and Tess joined them. The group
hugged. All the kids were dirty but happy.
"Sports day rules!" they shouted.

BEANBAG TOSS

You can play this sports day favourite in teams or one-on-one. Have fun indoors or outdoors!

What you need:
- 5 socks
- dried beans or rice
- scissors
- an empty container

What you do:
- To make the beanbags, fill each sock with dried beans or rice. Put the same amount in each sock. The beanbags should be about the size of an adult's fist.
- Tie a knot in each sock to close it. Cut off any extra material.
- Place the empty container on the other side of the room.
- Take turns throwing the beanbags into the container.
- The player who gets the most beanbags in wins!

REPLAY IT

Have another look at this picture. How do you think Stan felt when he fell? How would you feel?

Now pretend you are Stan. Write a thank-you note to Gigi for being such a good teammate.

ABOUT THE AUTHOR

Cari Meister is the author of more than 100 books for children. She lives with her family in Vail, Colorado, USA. She enjoys yoga, horseback riding and skiing.

ABOUT
THE ILLUSTRATOR

Seb Burnett is an illustrator and games developer living in Bristol. When he's not drawing, he loves going for long walks through the woods and hunting for monsters. He hasn't found any yet.